For Jan Walding - C.P.
For Leo - S.W.

First published in Great Britain in 2003
by Frances Lincoln Limited, 4 Torriano Mews,
Torriano Avenue, London NW5 2RZ

www.franceslincoln.com
www.carolinepitcher.co.uk

British Library Cataloguing in Publication Data available on request

ISBN 0-7112-2100-6

Set in Stone Serif

Printed in Singapore

1 3 5 7 9 8 6 4 2

THE WINTER
DRAGON

Caroline Pitcher ★ Sophy Williams

FRANCES LINCOLN

When winter came, Rory liked to stay inside
and play in his warm, bright house.

One day, Rory made a dragon. He painted him
emerald green. He gave him glitter eyes, an arrow tail
and a crest of brilliant red. When the dragon was dry,
Rory carried him upstairs and put him on his bed.

"Rory, time for sleep now," called his Mum.

Down came the big blanket of night, over all the things that Rory knew. He hid down in his bed. He hated the end of the day. He always thought monsters and demons of the dark might creep out from the shadows…

Then Rory heard a gentle growl and felt warm
breath upon his face. His room was lit by a glow,
green as an apple in deep magic. It was the dragon!

   "You're like a night-light," said Rory,
"but you haven't got a switch or a bulb."

   The dragon chuckled. "I shine to light the dark,
that's all. Don't fear the night while I am here."

   And he shone to keep the dark at bay.

The dragon's eyes gleamed red as he stood, arms folded, upon Rory's bed. His scales flashed like a knight's chain mail, and he lashed his tail!

He said, "I warmed your slippers, and your bed."

"You're like a hot water bottle," said Rory, "but you haven't got a stopper!"

The dragon chuckled. "I blow hot breath to warm things up, that's all. I am the Winter Dragon. Don't fear the cold while I am here."

And he stood guard over Rory as he drifted into sleep.

Each evening before bedtime,
the dragon came again.

"Please try a toasted teacake, Rory," he said,
crisping each half with his hot breath.
"I toast marshmallows and muffins, too."

"You'd be brilliant at a barbecue in summer!"
cried Rory. "We wouldn't need any charcoal
with you around!"

"I won't be here in the summer," said the dragon.

Later, when Rory had his bath,
the dragon blew to warm the water.
  "I don't take baths myself," he said.
"My fire might go out and my scales turn rusty."

"Listen, Rory," the dragon said, "I'll tell you stories
of when the world was young. I'll tell you about meteorites,
volcanoes and brilliant burning things, of fireworks and furnaces
and the great sizzling sun, of rubies deep inside the earth,
of garnet and of gold. I'll tell you stories of my family,
of Dinosaur, Lizard, and the Ancient Crocodile. They were so young
and soft-skinned when they came out of their eggs.
But they grew brave, Rory, just like you."

And in the dragon's dreamtime world, Rory did
grow brave. Dinosaur, Lizard and the Ancient
Crocodile became his dreamtime friends.

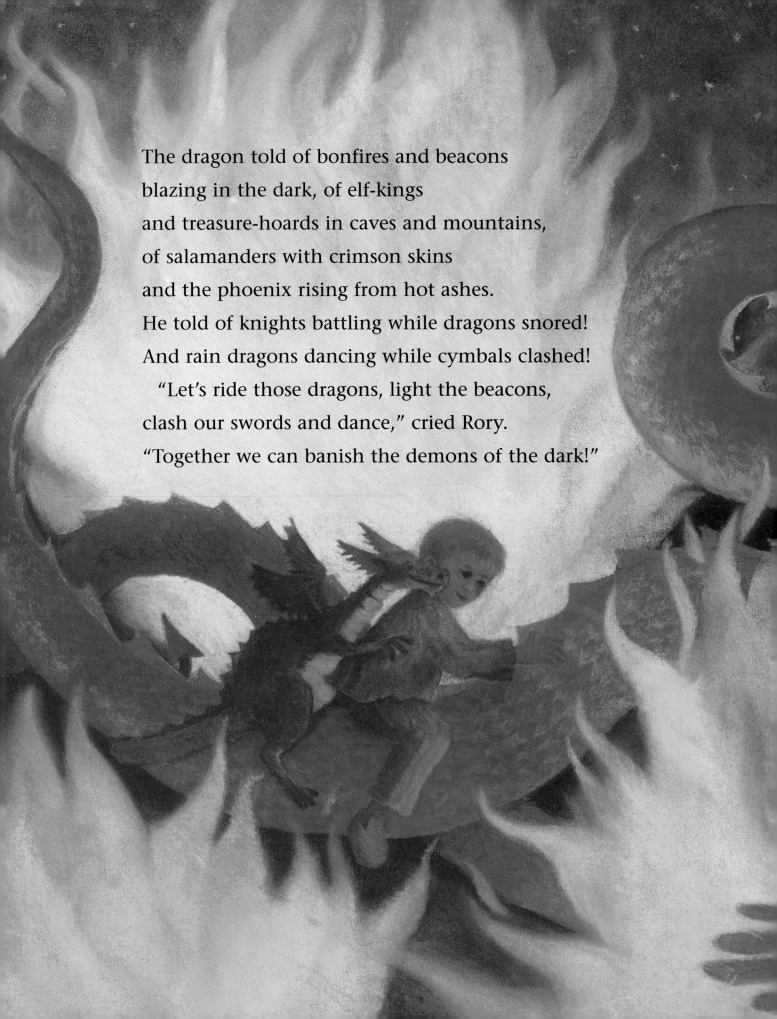

The dragon told of bonfires and beacons
blazing in the dark, of elf-kings
and treasure-hoards in caves and mountains,
of salamanders with crimson skins
and the phoenix rising from hot ashes.
He told of knights battling while dragons snored!
And rain dragons dancing while cymbals clashed!
 "Let's ride those dragons, light the beacons,
clash our swords and dance," cried Rory.
"Together we can banish the demons of the dark!"

And they did, and Rory slept peacefully till day.

"This dragon's getting scruffy," said Mum.

"The paint comes off in my hands. Shall we throw him out?"

"No!" cried Rory. "That's my Winter Dragon."

"We can't keep everything you make," she said.

"Just look at all these robots and old cars made of boxes."

"Take them then! But leave my dragon," said Rory.

The days grew longer and the sunlight stronger.
At night, Rory was asleep before night's black blanket fell.
He had the dragon's stories in his heart, and knew they would
protect him from the demons of the dark.

The daffodils burst open in the grass, but the dragon's colours
faded with the spring. His glitter eyes were dull. His crest had fallen
and Rory knew his dragon was longing to go home.

The next night the dragon was gone. Rory searched
and found him at the wood stove, gazing in.
His eyes were full of fire.

"That's my world, Rory," he said. "The melting middle
of the earth! See the golden centre and the blue-topped
flames. That's the place I love. It's time for me to go now.
I'll come back if ever you need me."

Spring and summer came and went, and when the winter
darkness fell again, Rory had warm memories to wear like
bright armour in the dark. He dreamed happily of his dragon,
at home in his own world of warmth and light.